This Sheriff Wags His Tail

By

William Aiello

PublishAmerica
Baltimore

ISBN: 978-1-4489-4984-7
PUBLISHED BY PUBLISHAMERICA, LLLP
www.publishamerica.com
Baltimore

Printed in the United States of America

Dean hadn't slept in two days. Fall was coming, the days were getting shorter, and his life, it seemed, was going nowhere.

For three weeks he'd been looking for a job. Four applications, three interviews, two rejections, one call not to come in, and no job. It was going to be hard in the coming months. New York winters can be rough, and the Farmer's Almanac predicted a severe one. Dean's unemployment was coming to an end, and he realized that the summer he spent hiking, biking and lazing around had been wasted. As a young boy, summers were his favorite season. But as an unemployed adult, they were a temptation.

He had just two months left and unemployment would expire. But there was more. The holidays were coming. Dean wanted dearly to visit his sister in suburban Omaha. Cheryl was his only sibling and he fiercely loved his two nephews and niece. But with the funds low and what seemed like a tough winter ahead, a visit as well as Christmas gifts seemed out of the question. For the first time, this was a Christmas season Dean felt he'd neither see his sister and her family nor give Jason, Stephanie and Christopher any gifts.

Holidays, in fact, didn't always bring joy to Dean's heart. Each Thanksgiving he'd remember the holiday eve in 1991 when the family got a call that cousin Greg had been killed in Iran. One month later, Dad had died unexpectedly, just three days before Christmas.

Holidays no longer meant to Dean what they once did. Was it just him, or did others get into low spirits when the Christmastide season came?

Cheryl was out in the Nebraska wilderness, as he called it. A strip mall and collection of modern home improvement stores did not make it seem cosmopolitan, at least not to him. But Dean's perception of life had changed in recent years. Since Mom died almost three years ago, he felt lonely and cold. Lisa, his last girlfriend, was out of his life also. She met some computer expert from down Baltimore way and took off.

This fall, it seemed, was more gloomy and gray than any other. The clouds rolling in over the mountains belied the sunny weather forecast for the next day.

Dean was alone, lonely and dispirited. In less than a year, he lost his job, his girlfriend and his verve. The glitter of the snow meant no more to him than the warm summer sunshine on the lake where he swam and played volleyball with his friends for years.

-1-

And so he dreaded the coming months more than he ever did before. The books he loved to read, the CDs of his favorite groups, the photo albums of good times stood against the wall like stiff wooden soldiers.

But what he really had to do was get a job. The economy was bad and he knew it wasn't going to be easy. Dean cursed the politicians whom he blamed for a lot of the mess both he and his town were in. He blamed both political parties and he blamed his neighbors who, he believed, seemed to care little about the situation. They had their sports, their beer, their cable television, all the other creature comforts...Dean cursed them for it.

There were all kinds of stories about Kinsford, two towns away, where illegal aliens were lured, putting some of the townspeople out of work. There had been a protest planned by some folks in the county to display their opposition, but not enough seemed to care and show up. It was planned as the same time as a televised football game, and that's what most of the citizens who planned to demonstrate watched that day.

Dean called it diversion apathy, and it made him real bitter.

And thus, at 38, Dean felt as if life had passed him by.

He thought over and over to himself. His parents were gone, Lisa had left him, he had no work. The only hope, as Dean saw it, was Cliff, a buddy he met when working at the video store three and a half years before. Cliff was his foreman, but also his friend. When a big video chain moved into the county, the small store could no longer compete. The place closed; both Dean and Cliff were out of work.

Cliff was the lucky soul. His work experience and aggressiveness got him a job at an investment firm. While there he was able to get an office with a view overlooking the Hudson River, and met Susan, whom he married.

Since Cliff got married, and became a father just over a year later, it wasn't the same. Cliff was still a friend, however. Dean went to the house about once a month. He loved getting out for a few hours, he loved discussing old times and movies. Cliff's son, Daniel, reminded him of Jason at that age. The bright blue eyes, thatched hair, and wide smile gave him a good feeling. And there was Leo, Cliff's Weimaraner. Dean loved dogs.

So this Saturday when Dean called Cliff, both knew this visit was going to be more than a social session. Dean needed help, and Cliff knew it.

It wasn't a long walk to Cliff's house. Cliff lived up the hill, past a small public park, and those visits were just about the only time Dean walked in that direction. In his school days, Dean had climbed the trees, knew every crack in the park sidewalk, knew which handball court he was more likely to play better at. Those once sharp memories had been buffed down to blurred images.

A summer passed, and Dean realized he had not stopped in the park once all season.

It was Saturday just after 3 PM. Dean felt the first slight, cool breeze, indicative of the real fall weather soon to come. The leaves on the trees were still green. Fall wasn't quite here yet.

Dean walked gingerly up the walk, recalling that one of the circular stones had been loose on the last visit. The chrysanthemums had only begun to bloom, and the sunshine was playing hide and seek behind the clouds.

Dean knocked on the door; Cliff answered within a few seconds. Daniel came into view right after that, his arms juggling a bottle, stuffed animal and toy car.

"You look tired," Cliff greeted him.

"I'm past tired," Dean replied.

Cliff took Dean straight to the living room. No small talk this time. No updates on events in town or what the local gossips have been discussing. Cliff didn't offer Dean coffee or a snack. He ordered Daniel to go to his room and play.

"I'm in a mess, Cliff. I don't know what to do."

Cliff looked at Dean, obliquely at first, then directly. He brought his lips together, almost beginning a sentence. Then Dean resumed the talk.

"Are there any jobs at your company? I'll do anything, work in the mailroom, answer emails. Come on, Cliff, I'm your friend."

Dean knew Cliff couldn't give him a straight answer.

"I'm not the personnel director, Dean. I give people investment advice. Didn't I tell you when the video store closed to take a course and get your license?"

Dean didn't answer. For just a few seconds he kept quiet, but it seemed like hours. During those couple of seconds both the room and the outdoors appeared to grow darker. And silent.

Cliff knew Dean well enough that he had little ambition. But he felt it best to repeat the words he'd told Dean several times before. Not so much as advice, but preparation for the conversations he might have someday with his own son.

"Dean, you're not going to-"

But Dean cut him off.

"You have clients, lots of people from the area who are in business. Doesn't someone have a job for me?"

And the silence returned. Only this time it was Cliff who felt the time stand still and the environment get darker.

They just looked at each other. Cliff once felt like a father to Dean, giving him pep talks and advice. But Cliff had a son now, and looked upon his former coworker as a student he once taught. What stood in Cliff's way was that he liked Dean, and couldn't send the guy away with very harsh words.

Cliff got up first, sighed a deep breath, and put a hand on his former coworker's shoulder.

"Look, Dean-guy." Dean-guy was the name he used affectionately only on those occasions when Cliff felt Dean had done well or made a smart move. This time it was different.

"The people who come to the company are clients." He paused for a few minutes. "They are clients. I can't ask them for a job. It's like going to a foot doctor when someone else has the pain."

He paused again. Then he got more serious, put a hand on the shoulder again, but then removed it and looked Dean squarely in the eye.

"If I hear of something, I'll tell you. But you're the one looking for the job. I can't do it for you, Dean. You have to. It's your life."

Dean stared into space for what seemed like an hour. The room got darker than it ever was. Cliff's silhouette was completely stationary. Dean switched palms from knee to knee, then he rose, nodded, and realized Cliff was right. He had to do it for himself.

Dean had been spoiled. For most of his life, he had people to rely on. After Mom passed away, he was alone for the first time. In the past he had his parents, his sister, friends, Lisa, and a job to keep him occupied. Now he had no one. Mom didn't leave him as big an inheritance as he expected. She left some of the estate to her sister. He was alone. All alone.

Cliff offered Dean a drink, and said if he'd like, would ask Susan to save a place for him at dinner.

But Dean declined. He had asked enough of Cliff. It was time to go.

Dean spent only about half an hour at Cliff's home, but it felt much longer. It was a lot darker outside and the fall breeze blew harder and cooler. The chrysanthemums waved in the breeze as a few leaves fell from a tree. Not quite 4 PM, the thick cloud cover made it feel like evening. Only a spark of a sun ray peeked through a tiny break in the clouds.

Standing in the doorway, Dean looked up at that spark. It seemed to smile at him and beckon him outdoors.

"Good luck, Dean-guy." Cliff beamed, a spark in his eye matched the flicker in the sky he saw just a minute before.

"Call me sometime. There's still time for a hike or a bicycle ride in the mountains before winter arrives."

Dean left and discerned both his relationship with Cliff and the future would never be the same. He had to take charge of his life.

The walk back home was different than the way he came. He took the long walk through the park. Going past the swings, benches and a small garden, he slowly realized that he had not been to this section since his high school days. He recalled climbing the monkey bars with Jimmy, Leo and Joey. He could picture being on the swings with his sister. He could still imagine a park employee planting the bushes in the garden.

For the first time in at least two decades he sat down on the bench. Within a few minutes he was oblivious to the breeze, the leaves falling, and the chrysanthemums swaying. Dean's mind drifted back and forth from his younger days to the discussion he had with Cliff. He lost all track of the time and he no longer felt any temperature nor was he conscious of any sensation around him. All he saw were shadows, images, patterns...And then, in a moment, he returned to reality, as he heard rustling and commotion in the bushes.

Dean came back to the world around him and saw that night had arrived without warning him. The lights were on in the lampposts, as he became aware that he had been dreaming longer than he made notice of.

The rustle in the bushes continued. Dean had lived here long enough to presume it was either a prairie dog or a neighborhood cat. But slowly a figure emerged from the bushes and chrysanthemums. It was a small dog, a puppy. It seemed to wag its tail as it found Dean, its eyes glimmered from the lantern lights. As puppies do, it approached Dean, first sniffing around his shoes, jauntily bouncing, as only a puppy can do. He had fortunately discovered a human, and tried jumping on Dean's lap.

Dean was a bit apprehensive, although the pup seemed completely harmless. He wanted to pet the little guy, but hesitated. Four times the dog jump on Dean, and four times he was placed on the ground. Finally, he sat down, cheerfully looked up at Dean, almost saying, go ahead, pet me. And so, his newfound friend did. With an older dog Dean would have been afraid, but this little guy wanted a friend. And so did Dean.

It was dark, yet his shiny black coat and sparkling eyes were enough for Dean to recognize him as a Labrador retriever. But where did he come from?

There wasn't a soul in the park, nor anyone nearby. From the looks of the little critter he didn't appear malnourished or injured.

"Come up here, little fella," Dean motioned to the dog, and extended an arm to the bench. This pup needed no second command. He knew exactly what to do. Jumping on the bench, and onto Dean's lap, the little guy seemed perfectly content. So did Dean. For the first time in months, a wide beam came across his face.

It was strange indeed. Since Lisa's departure, he hadn't been very happy. There were no smiles in his voice when he telephoned Cheryl, and he left Cliff's home very disappointed. And here, in an instant, a dog comes out of the bushes and lights up his life.

"You're a cute little guy. Oh, you know that." His tail was wagging merrily.

"So, what's your name, huh? Who do you belong to?" The puppy just kept wagging his tail, jumping, and looking straight into Dean's eyes.

It was by now well past 7 PM and Dean was both cold and hungry. He had always loved animals, and one of the good things about where he was living is that pets were permitted. This little fellow had no license and no collar; obviously he was lost. Or maybe some cruel person didn't want to care for him and just let him loose.

"Okay, little guy, you know what? You're coming home with me."

It was almost as if this dog understood, as he licked Dean's face and jumped to the ground to begin the trek home.

"Somebody is looking for you, I'll bet. But we can't worry about that now. You can come home with me.

Tomorrow we'll start searching for your owner."

Somehow, the walk home didn't seem as long. Dean got to his front door with his new pal by his side. This was a puppy, but he was no shy guest.

Dean opened the door and his four legged new friend made himself comfortably at home. The little guy sniffed around the furniture, jumped on the easy chair, and after inspecting each room, sat on the living room rug. With the dog's tail wagging, Dean knew the animal was looking for something to eat.

"I'm afraid there isn't any dog food, young guy. You'll have to wait until tomorrow when I can go to the store. Let's see what I've got for you in the house."

Dean put together a concoction of crackers, half a frankfurter, and a leftover burger from a fast food restaurant. But the puppy didn't mind. He ate it in no time.

"Listen, young man," Dean looked directly at him as if the dog was a student and he a counselor. "You're here for the night. Tomorrow I've got to find who you belong to and return you to your owner. I'm sure someone is looking for you."

But all the little guy had in mind was someone to give him attention. His tail wagged like a leaf in the wind. Each time he looked at Dean, it virtually resembled a smile, as if they'd been friends for years.

Dean picked the little guy up and held him way above his head. "You've probably got a name. Only I don't know it."

He thought for a moment. "I'm going to call you Sonny. You are someone's son. And although it's spelled another way, you sure brought some sunshine into my day."

But the sun outside had long since set. It was getting late. "I've got to find your master."

That would wait until the next day. Dean pondered where to put Sonny for the night and whether he'd sleep or stay up all night running around or chewing shoes.

Dean had an old wicker basket in the closet. He put a partly worn blanket down in it and a bowl of water alongside. That was the easy part. The rough part was whether his new little friend would take the hint and sleep in the bed Dean made for him.

He turned the lights down a bit and put the puppy into the basket. To his surprise Sonny lied down.

Relieved, Dean showered and thought maybe it wasn't such a bad day after all. That morning he awoke feeling as he did every morning, that it would be another dull, aimless day, hoping that some unexpected excitement might occur. By the time he left Cliff's house, it was another dreary day, just different circumstances. Then a little pup comes into his life and made him feel really good.

Dean stepped out of the bath expecting to find his house guest fast asleep. A peek into the bedroom and the basket was empty. He searched high and low all over the bedroom, under the beds, in closets. No Sonny.

Knowing puppies just love to eat, Dean felt most likely his friend wandered into the kitchen. Nope, no dog.

This narrowed the search down a bit. There wasn't much of the apartment left to rummage. He turned the light on and voila'—there was Sonny, lying on the couch.

Lounging comfortably, but not asleep.

Still wet from the shower, Dean lifted his little buddy, and the tail went into over-wag again.

"Look, little guy. You're my guest here. A guest doesn't take advantage of his host. Besides, by tomorrow at this time you'll probably be back with your owner. Don't think that because you're so cute that you're going to get away with things."

Dean went into the bedroom and put Sonny back into the wicker basket. He took all his shoes and put them in the closet, just in case the puppy felt like a midnight meal. Then he closed the door, so the dog wouldn't sneak out.

Dean dried himself, made a small snack, and thought of his plans for the next day. That will be Sunday, usually a day he had for himself. However, this Sunday, he'd have to find Sonny's owner.

Dean finished his snack and went into the bedroom. He turned on the light and...an empty wicker basket. No dog anywhere. Dean felt Sonny had to be under the bed. But no dog there either. As he lifted himself, Dean felt a soft mass under the blanket of his bed. A soft, warm, pulsing mass, with a cold snout and tail sticking out. There was Sonny, having a sweet dream on Dean's bed.

Dean took the puppy and gently placed him back into the bed he made for him. Sonny stayed for a few seconds, then leaped back on the bed.

Dean didn't lose patience, he found it all amusing. This little guy obviously wanted a closer position to his master's bed. So Dean took the wicker basket and moved it right to the foot of the bed. That seemed to please Sonny, he looked up at Dean and gave a doggie smile. Dean put him in a sleeping position.

It didn't last long. Sonny got up and jumped on Dean's bed. Dean realized any type of negotiation would not work.

If Sonny wanted to stay on the bed, then he won the battle. Besides, Dean believed, it's just for one night.

-2-

The sunlight peeked through the blinds as Dean began to come out of his slumber. For just a second he forgot that he had an overnight guest, but looking on the bed there was Sonny right next to him.

As Dean alighted from the bed, Sonny was right behind him. The dog followed him as Dean washed, opened the blinds, and dressed.

"You're hungry little guy, I know it. Puppies never have enough to eat, huh?" Dean picked him up and again the tail waved back and forth at record speed.

Sonny kept looking at Dean.

"You know what, I'm hungry, too. How about we have breakfast together?"

Dean finished dressing. He didn't have a leash, but he had a long rope, tied a few rubberbands, and took his pal out for a walk.

Returning home, Dean didn't know what to feed his furry pal. He cut up a few pieces of bread.

"You like cereal, guy? That's what I usually begin my day with. I'm afraid you're going to have to accept it. Haven't got anything else for you."

Dean heated milk, added cereal, and the cut bread, then fed Sonny. He wasn't sure the puppy would go for it.

"Well, here goes. I hear puppies will eat anything. Hope you like it."

Within a few minutes, the pup finished the bowl clean.

Dean made his own breakfast, finished dressing, and planned his day.

"You know what, little guy? I've got to find your owner. Somebody must be looking for you. But you might be here a while, so I've got to get you some food, too."

Dean found an old box in the apartment. Then he went into the yard and collected a few others from among the boxes the super got deliveries in. He assembled a makeshift cage, punched holes in it, left a bowl of water, and carefully placed Sonny inside.

It wasn't far from a grocery store and a pet shop. Along the way, Dean looked for signs about a lost puppy. He asked a few folks if they knew of anyone who had lost a dog, but no luck. He was short on money, but had to feed his friend. He felt that if the owner showed up, he could easily sell the remaining food.

Dean bought a few groceries for himself as well, and headed home. He walked on the opposite side of the street, looking for lost dog posters, and again asked a few townspeople whether they heard any news of a missing pet.

Arriving home, Dean heard wailing sounds as he entered the lobby of the small apartment building he lived in. He knew immediately what the sounds were.

One neighbor came out of her apartment. "I saw you coming into the lobby. If you got a pet, you better keep him quiet." And she slammed the door.

Going into his apartment, the yelp was a lot louder than it was in the hallway.

Dean was in deep thought for a few moments. His act of humanity may not go over so well with his neighbors. Who else heard the constant noise? While pets were allowed where he lived, excessive noise wasn't.

He returned to reality. He entered the bedroom and the yelps ceased. The cage was opened, and Sonny sprung out, into Dean's arms, licking and kissing him. The tail was wagging happily.

But it wasn't without a signal. Sonny looked at him, almost admonishing Dean that he ought not to leave him alone for so long. Then in a second it was over.

The realization came to Dean that he better make sure Sonny wasn't a nuisance. Yet there was a possibility of more episodes. Dean had to leave for business and to shop, he needed to find a job, and who knows how long before the pup's owner was located. He sure couldn't leave a dog not housebroken with a neighbor.

Well, it wasn't worth dwelling on, or so he thought.

"Listen, little guy. I bought you some dog food and doggie biscuits." Sonny's tail went into overdrive and he feigned a dog smile.

"But I've got to find your owner, only nobody so far seems to have lost a pooch. I don't know what to do. Do you?"

Sonny tilted his head the way dogs do when they don't comprehend completely.

A light bulb came on. Dean got the idea of posting notices around town. That might locate the owner.

Dean found some colored pieces of construction paper. He took out a few big markers, gave it a few minutes of contemplation, and in big, neat letters he wrote:

LOST PUPPY

BLACK LAB

FOUND IN CHERRYWOOD PARK

CALL 555-4494

He designed nine notices. One for the supermarket, one for the bank. Another for the post office, one each for the medical clinic and the Y. The remainder he'd post on telephone poles or bus shelters.

It was almost lunch time when the telephone rang. Strange, Dean felt. He seldom got calls on a Sunday, and it was too early for Cheryl to call.

Dean picked up. "Hello."

"It's Cliff, Dean. Am at my job. You know I work some Sundays. Can't talk long. There might be work for you. A medical office in the next town. The doctor is moving to larger quarters. He needs someone to paint and move furniture. Here's the number if you're interested..."

Dean wrote the number quickly and called. The man who answered was the doctor who owned the practice. He was Dr. Wainer. Yes, indeed, someone was needed to paint and move equipment.

"I've got three guys to move furniture and paint a couple of rooms. It's just a small job. I need one more man. Can you paint?"

"Sure can," Dean replied at once.

"Well, I'd like to meet you first and discuss the job. Can you get here this afternoon?" Dr. Wainer gave him the address and told him what time to be there.

"Great. I'll be there at 2 PM." It wasn't steady work, but if he got it, it was a job. Dean got a rush of optimism.

The bus leaving town would take him two blocks away from the doctor's office. And it would be a perfect opportunity for him to post more lost dog notices.

He made a quick lunch, fed the dog, and got the posters together. He left well over an hour before the interview time. Doesn't look good to be late for a job interview.

"Hey, little guy, wish me luck. He paused. "Say, if I get the job, you might get a steak for dinner or a dish of pasta."

Dean was on his way out, then remembered the neighbor angry that the dog had howled while he was away earlier that morning. Dean couldn't give him the free run of the house. Sonny wasn't housebroken. But he might also stay by the door and wail the whole time he was alone. Then Dean remembered the time when he was a young boy and his grandfather had a clever idea how to keep a dog quiet and occupied when alone.

He reassembled the makeshift cage and poured fresh water in the bowl. Finally, he added a ticking alarm clock to keep the puppy company.

Placing the dog gingerly in the box, the pup seemed fascinated with the alarm clock. He sniffed at it and seemed to be in tune with the ticking. Dean couldn't wait more than a few moments. But he felt satisfied that Sonny had an object that would pacify him and keep the critter from annoying the neighbors. Feeling proud of his idea, he left the apartment and went to the direction of the bus station.

On his way, he passed a bank, supermarket and the Y. Using his ATM card, he went inside the bank and posted a sign. He did the same on the supermarket bulletin board and at the Y. He got to the bus stop and there was one passenger waiting. The woman looked at him as Dean pondered whether or not to hang a sign. After asking the woman if she knew anyone who lost a dog and getting her negative reply, he hung a sign at the depot. Her initial stern demeanor turned into appreciation as she commended him for his thoughtfulness.

Luck was with him up to this point. The bus came almost immediately after he posted the sign. He smiled to himself and felt a sense of accomplishment and hope. The rest of the day goes as smoothly as it has so far, he'll arrive in plenty of time for the interview and he might just have a job.

It wasn't 1:15 yet, so Dean had a few minutes to look around . He hadn't been to this part of town in quite some time. It had changed indeed. For a Sunday it was bustling and crowded, not the way he remembered it the last time he was here. A new fast food restaurant, an office building, stationery store. But also a few abandoned and empty storefronts. It was pretty obvious to him the bad economy and high rents had kept many businesses from renting or forced some to close.

But right now the job was his priority. He walked straight to the office address he was given.

Dean went up the stairs and rang the bell. A man answered as Dean asked for Dr. Wainer.

"I'm Dr. Wainer. A fiftyish man with salt and pepper wavy hair and round frame glasses answered. "Come in, please"

Dr. Wainer took Dean to a room in the rear of the office. "You're probably a little surprised that I'm here on a Sunday. I'd like to get my new office painted and the furniture moved as soon as possible."

"I'm Dean. I called you about the job to paint and move furniture."

Dr. Wainer smiled faintly. "Oh, yes, I forgot to ask your name."

The doctor asked him to sit and to pardon the appearance and condition of the room. It was long and narrow, with a ceiling lamp.

"As you can see, I'm preparing to move out. Need to be in the new place by the end of the week. I've got three men. Need one more. Can you paint?"

Dean took the bull by the horns. "Sure. I painted my apartment and my cousin's attic."

"Good. There is office furniture that has to be moved also."

"Where is it going?"

"There's a new office building two blocks away. Actually, the furniture is there. I'm cleaning out old files here. You and the other three men will have to move it into place after the paint job. Can you do it?"

"Sure. Just tell me when to start."

Dean thought for a second, it was the new office building he passed on the way to the interview.

Dr. Wainer continued. "A doctor is moving out. He was only there one year. Rent is very high. So I'm moving in. It's a six room office. The whole office doesn't need painting. Just a few rooms, some touch-up work, shelves, closets, and the window frames."

Dean gave a slow look at the old fashioned decor of the present office and could see the doctor's reasons for relocating. "I believe I passed the office on the way here."

The doctor nodded approvingly and seemed to like Dean's familiarity with the section of town. "I can take you there. Two blocks away."

Dean recalled Cliff's words that he needed to take command of his life. "I'll be glad to do the work for you, doctor."

It was a brief walk to the doctor's new headquarters. Dr. Wainer showed Dean the office and exactly what needed to be painted as well as where the furniture would be positioned.

"Very good. Can you start tomorrow?"

"I'm ready to start any day."

Dr. Wainer beamed. "Excellent. I'll be in the new office tomorrow at 9 AM. That's when you'll start. You'll paint first, then move the furniture as I explain. I think it can all be done in two days"

The doctor discussed what he'd pay. He shook Dean's hand briskly. "Tomorrow, nine o'clock. Please be on time."

Dean nodded noticeably, and bid the doctor good afternoon. Dean was elated. He found work, if only for two days. He walked to the bus depot for the return trip home.

Walking into the lobby of his apartment building, he heard the familiar caterwaul. It was Sonny. Not as bad or as steady as the morning, but audible nonetheless.

He climbed the stairs to his apartment, and opened the door. Mr. and Mrs. Krady appeared in the doorway of their apartment, which is next to his. Dean had had an argument with them before, and from the look on Mr. Krady's face, Dean knew what to expect.

You got a pet?" Krady screamed.

Dean nodded.

"You better keep that animal quiet. He's been crying all afternoon. My wife is ill and can't rest. You keep him quiet or I'll have the landlord make you get rid of him."

Krady went into his apartment and the loud slam of the door shook the walls.

Dean knew this time that the matter was serious. Krady wasn't someone to mess with. He had a reputation for being a tough guy, and despite being in his seventies, could easily take care of himself. The previous winter Krady went fisticuffs with a local drunk who'd slip into the building on cold nights and sleep in the alcove in the hall.

Besides, what other neighbors heard the noise? Had anyone already gone to the landlord and complained? Some of the joy he'd gotten from getting a job had evaporated as he thought about a possible warning from the landlord.

Now he had a new dilemma. He was scheduled to work the next day. But what about the dog? The following day he'd be gone for at least nine hours. Sonny was sure to wail. Dean had to think and act fast. His only hope was Cliff.

Dean called Cliff and thanked him for the job opportunity. Cliff was happy to know that Dean had found work. He was glad to have helped his buddy.

Then Dean mentioned the dog he had found returning home from Cliff's house the day before.

Cliff didn't know of anyone who lost a puppy. But Dean's real request was for someone to care for the dog while he was at work for maybe two days. He explained how the dog yelped and barked when left alone.

There was silence on the end of the line for almost a minute. Before Cliff spoke, Dean volunteered a soft but honest "Please." He was anticipating a negative response, but Cliff agreed to babysit the dog.

"Okay, I sort of owe it to you. I told you about the job. Even though I wasn't aware that you had the dog. But just a few days, you hear?"

Dean was delighted and so thankful.

"Thanks, Cliff. That's two I owe you."

-3-

Sunday evening came pretty quickly. Dean found old clothes to paint in and put them aside so they'd be ready for Monday morning.

Then he got together all of Sonny's equipment—the wicker basket, water dish, blankets. He took the cans of dog food and placed them in a bag. Then he placed his furry little friend in the basket and the two of them left, heading for Cliff's house.

"Listen, little guy. I have to work the next few days."

They went out the building, down the block, and through the stone path of the park.

Dean knocked and Cliff answered immediately. Cliff gave a broad smile, welcomed Dean in. From the look on Cliff's face, he clearly found the pup adorable.

Taking the retriever puppy out of the basket, Cliff extended his arms and quickly took hold of the dog.

"He sure is cute."

"I said that the second I saw him. It's funny, I found him coming home from here on Saturday. Now I'm here again, with the little guy found after leaving here. When I left, my life was pretty bad. Now I've got a new friend and a job."

Dean didn't prolong the conversation, he had to go. Cliff promised to take good care of the dog.

"The paint job ought to be done by Wednesday. I'll call you when I'm ready to pick him up."

Cliff was a bit puzzled. "You plan to keep this dog?"

"I don't know." Dean hesitated for a few moments. "I'd like to, but he barks and whines a lot. If I get full time work, can't leave him alone all day. A couple of neighbors have complained."

Cliff shook his head in agreement.

Dean hesitated a few more seconds. "I posted a few signs around here. When I'm in town this week, will hang a few more. Sure would like to know where this dog came from. He looks like he was cared for. He must belong to someone. But if and when his owner does show up, I'll certainly miss him. Just two days, and I'm really attached to him."

Cliff wished Dean well on the job, and he left for home. They bade each other goodnight. Cliff could see he was happy to have found work. Cliff also knew that Dean had been alone a long time, and the dog was not just good company, but gave him someone to spend his time with. Cliff could never stop thinking of Dean as a son sometimes. Or maybe a younger brother. Cliff new Dean well, probably better than anyone else. Despite the joy over finding work and a puppy, Dean wasn't all together. Cliff could discern that. Something was still on Dean's mind.

After Dean departed, Cliff realized once more why he stayed friends with him and how much he silently admired the man. A lot of people would probably have just ignored the puppy and left him in the park. Dean had a heart, he just had a funny way of showing it most of the time.

Dean was walking home, on the way passing two signs he had posted about a lost puppy. One was partially ripped. Dean cursed, but not as angry as he had been a week before. Probably some heartless soul or smart aleck teenagers tried to take it down.

Home again, it was the first night in what seemed like ages that he had to arise early the next morning. He made four more posters about a lost puppy.

-4-

The alarm rang before sunrise. Dean dressed and got himself ready. He had nearly forgotten the early morning ritual of going to work. He gathered the set of old clothes and hat which he put aside the night before.

He was the second person at the bus depot, glimpsing and gazing at the workday crowd he had not been a part of for quite some time. It seemed like ages since he waited at this depot to go to work, as he anxiously waited for the bus to arrive. Looking up and around, with the leaves on the trees in fall colors and chrysanthemums planted by the county government which were not there the last time he worked, some changes had occurred since the last time he waited here to go to work. The day before, his mind was preoccupied by the job interview, and he had no sense to notice the flowers or the new bus shelter. Today, he did.

Again, the bus came pretty quickly. Rush hours were different. He needed a seat with enough room to place his bag.

It took longer to get downtown than Sunday when he went for the interview. On the way to the office, he tacked posters for a lost dog. One on a telephone pole, one on a lamp post, one in the post office,   and one in the bulletin board of a convenience store.

Dean arrived at the office location where Dr. Wainer was talking to two others who'd be painting with him. In a few minutes the fourth painter arrived.

The doctor asked them to introduce themselves. It would be Rick, Al, Jim and Dean. Then he explained why four painters had been hired. "I need to be out of my present office and in here by next week. Two rooms don't need any work. Four rooms, plus closets, baseboards and window frames. Each one of you gets a room. All the paint, rollers, and brushes are here. Two fifteen minute breaks and forty minutes for lunch. One of you men finishes, help another. I'll be in my old office two blocks away if you have any questions. My number is in the cabinet if you need to call. Call me at the end of the day so I can lock up."

The painters discussed who'd do which room, who'd get the ladders first, who was better at closets, and so on.

By the end of the first day, most of the work was finished and they congratulated each other on a job well done.

Rick and Dean became friends during the day. After the job, they went out for a snack. It was such a long time since Dean was with anyone he could classify as a friend, except Cliff. He almost forgot what it was like.

They went to a restaurant two blocks from the doctor's office. A cozy little place with decorative tablecloths and light green curtains. Plus a small community bulletin board. Dean took his last notice about the lost dog and posted it.

Rick and Dean ordered their food. Rick asked Dean what he had posted on the board.

"Oh, a notice about a lost puppy. I found him last Saturday. Or maybe he found me. A Labrador retriever. Cute little guy. He came up to me in Cherrywood Park. I couldn't leave him homeless, so took him home. I'm posting signs around town. Hope his owner sees one and calls me."

The conversation turned to other topics. Rick and Dean discussed family, past girlfriends and prior jobs they had.

Dean had to get going. While there was still time before the last bus left the depot, Dean didn't want to wait on a long line.

Rick lived in a town in the opposite direction and offered Dean a ride home, but Dean declined. He didn't want to take advantage of someone he just met.

Dean got on the bus and used the travel time to daydream about the work he had finished. Usually he reflected on his abysmal future, but the paint job gave him something more pleasant to think about.

He got home and called Cliff. The dog was fine. Cliff was really enjoying the puppy. He loved canines as much as Dean. And Cliff's son was enjoying the pup as well.

The next morning came quickly and early. Dean eagerly dressed and prepared himself for the day. Having made a friend with Rick, he felt a little more optimistic about the day ahead of him.

There was still a little time before the bus would come, so he took out more sheets of oak tag, and made three more signs about a lost dog.

Dean put his jacket on and with the three signs walked energetically to the bus station. Although he left at the same time as the day before, there was a difference in the air and atmosphere. It was chillier than Monday, but the sun shone brighter. The sparkling sunshine reflected off the colorful fall foliage and smiled upon the marigolds and chrysanthemums that survived this late into the season.

The bus was waiting at the depot, but Dean swiftly hung a notice about the dog on a telephone booth a block before. The ride into town seemed to go faster than on

Monday, even with more passengers on board. Again, he fell into a daydream, but was alert enough to know when it was time to disembark.

Leaving the bus, he stopped into the shop for a cup of coffee. It was where he and Rick had a snack the night before. Almost at once he noticed the sign about the dog had been removed.

But there was no time to think about it. He had a job to get to.

Dr. Wainer was at the office and Dean was the first of the four painters to arrive. In a somber and low tone, the doctor beckoned good morning and told Dean to get into his work clothes. "I'll tell you more when the other men get here."

Then the doctor paused and looked around, inspecting the work done the day prior. Dean was expecting criticism. Dr. Wainer didn't seem pleased.

"You guys did a pretty good job. Do the baseboards last."

Again a pause. The doctor was about to speak again when Rick and Al came in. Within a minute, the fourth and last man, Jim, was present also.

The boss called them in together. "You men did pretty well. I hope you can finish by today. Do the baseboards and moldings last. Call me if you finish early. I'll pay you for the whole day."

Dr. Wainer was a man of few words and half grins. He said no more and he was out.

The four men divided the balance of the work to be done among themselves. Not strangers like the day before, they felt more comfortable with each other and Jim asked if anyone minded that he had brought a radio. They chose a station of common like and the work day began.

It was just after 2 PM when the last window frame was painted. Rick called Dr. Wainer who said that he'd be there in a quarter of an hour.

The cool breeze helped to dry the paint which sparkled as it came through the drapeless windows.

The doctor arrived and seemed satisfied with the work. He went in and out of each room, checking the final look, flicking light switches on and off. A nod, a very brief smile, a few times he brought his lips together and tightened his chin.

"Good job, men!" He showed where to move furniture. "Okay, clean up, put the canvas and ladders in one room and come down to my office two blocks away." He gave them the key to lock.

Dean felt fairly good that Dr. Wainer was satisfied. He hadn't done painting in a long time. But like riding a bicycle, it all came back to him.

Dean, Rick, Al and Jim walked together to the doctor's present quarters. He gave them their pay envelopes, thanked them, and wished them well.

They only worked together two days, but went out after the work was completed to celebrate a job well done. Dean and Rick suggested the restaurant from the night before.

Walking in, Dean again noticed that the sign he had posted was gone. After placing his order, he spoke to the man behind the deli counter about it.

"Some woman came in this morning and took it off. I don't know who she was. Seen her in here a few times. That's all I know."

Dean pondered for a second. He moved his eyes from one side to the other, but any thoughts did not last long. Some of his signs closer to home were ripped off as well.

The men had a hearty meal and said their goodbyes. Again, Rick offered Dean a ride, but Dean declined. They shook hands and hoped for a reunion sometime in the future.

The bus was waiting as Dean got to the station, and he took the last available seat. The ride home was quick and smooth. Again, he daydreamed on his ride home, but before he knew it the bus had come to his stop to get off.

He walked happily to his home, for the first time in months he had earned a few day's pay. Into his apartment, and something else also for the first time in months: a message on his answering machine.

It's probably Cliff, he thought. Although curious someone called him, he was in no real hurry to answer. He put his clothes away, after which he pressed the button to hear the message.

"I'm calling about the sign for the lost dog. Uh...my name is Katie. I lost a Labrador retriever pup last week. It was on Rockline Avenue. I'd like to see the dog to know if he's mine. I named him Sheriff because he seemed to be boss of the house as soon as I took him home. My number is 555-9011."

Dean was shocked to hear it. But suddenly remembered the man at the deli counter explaining a woman took the sign down.

He called the number and a voice like that on the tape answered.

"May I speak with Katie?"

"This is Katie."

"You left a message about a lost dog."

"Yes, I did. Is he there?"

"Well, describe him."

"Mine was a black Lab puppy. His name is Sheriff."

"It is a black Lab, but he's not here right now. I worked today and left him with a friend. I can get him tomorrow and you can come here to see if he's yours."

"That will be great!" Katie was almost ecstatic.

"I'll get him from my friend Cliff and you can be here tomorrow. How's that?"

"Oh, that's just wonderful. I miss him so much and thought he was gone forever. By the way, thanks so much for posting the sign. Oh, one more thing, what's your name?"

"I'm Dean. Like Dean Martin. Only I don't sing."

Katie laughed. "I'll call you tomorrow. How is three o'clock?"

"Three o'clock is cool. Call me tomorrow."

"Okay, and thanks again."

Dean quickly called Cliff and explained the situation. An appointment was made for Dean to go to Cliff's house early in the morning to get the dog. "I'm sure going to miss the puppy," Cliff exclaimed. "He's absolutely adorable."

-5-

Morning came and Dean made a quick breakfast. He headed to Cliff's home, walking through the park where the dog he named Sonny first appeared in his life just over three days before.

Cliff was at this job, but his wife let Dean in. Dean spoke briefly with Susan. He had always gotten along with her. Susan could see that having a job for two days did a lot of good for Dean's outlook and spirits. Susan held the puppy for one last time and a slight tear developed in her eye as she handed him over.

"He's the cutest little dog, I'll tell you that. We loved having him here. But we're glad his owner called. He'll go back to his home." Susan also gave Dean the basket, dish, blankets, and what was left of the dog food. Susan provided one of several leashes they had.

"Here, this will make it a little easier taking him home. You can give it back to us later."

She pet the dog one final time.

Dean was fairly content, much more so than he had been in many months. In just a few days, he had found work, made a friend with Rick, found a puppy, and possibly did a good deed by locating the puppy's owner. His spirits hadn't been so cheerful in such a long time.

But it was short-lived. Walking into the ground floor of his apartment building, Mr. Barlett, the owner and landlord, was spraying cleanser on the windows.

Barlett looked at him intensely. "So you do have a dog."

Dean didn't answer.

"I've had some complaints about you and the dog. He's been making noise, barking and crying. A lot of people are complaining."

Dean knew Mr. Barlett well after living here so many years. Barlett made a big issue of every little item and exaggerated about nearly everything.

This time Dean retorted rapidly. "I'm pretty sure Krady was the only one who said anything. He barks more than the dog."

After so many years, Dean could handle Barlett.

"Krady probably told you the dog was barking non-stop, every day for the last week."

"He did."

Krady's a liar. He whined for a couple of hours two days. The dog wasn't here the last two days."

"But you-"

Dean cut him off. "You can relax. His owner is coming for him this afternoon. And you can tell Krady to get his facts straight."

Dean didn't always use his brain, but he knew how to handle Barlett. The landlord wasn't mean at heart, he just had to let people know he was boss. Plus, the events of the last few days gave Dean renewed conviction.

Nothing more was said. He went into his apartment. Dean made himself lunch and fed the dog, for what he believed would be the last meal they'd share together.

"Hey, little guy, do you know someone named Katie? She says she's your owner. She'll be here in a little while to take you home."

Dean recalled that Katie named the dog Sheriff. He picked the dog up, smiled at him, then put him down on the floor and let him run around the house. Then he yelled out the name Sheriff.

The pup stopped and turned around. Yes, indeed, Katie likely was the owner.

Dean tidied the house up and had just finished a snack when Katie telephoned. He told her that the dog was there and her voice brightened. She was given the address and she stated that she'd be there within an hour.

It was eleven minutes after three o'clock when the doorbell rang. Dean buzzed her in and a feeling of accomplishment overwhelmed him.

She knocked on the door and Dean opened. Katie was beaming, her brown hair partly hidden under a red knit hat. Dean smiled brilliantly. For a few seconds he was speechless and forgot his composure. Then he regained and asked Katie in.

"Is he here?"

"Oh, yeah. Of course."

Dean opened the bedroom door and the Labrador retriever galloped into Katie's arms. Licking and kissing her, Dean saw how happy both were.

"Sheriff, I'm so thrilled to see you again. I thought you were gone forever."

Sheriff's tail was wagging wildly. He continued to kiss and lick the owner he was reunited with.

"Well, I guess I don't have to ask if you're his owner."

Katie took her hat off and got semi-serious. "I don't know how to thank you. It's really thoughtful and humane what you did."

Dean tried to speak several times but the right words just didn't come. Then without any forethought, "It's funny, I called him Sonny. But he never really answered to it. How old is he?"

"Seven months. He was just three weeks old when I got him. A lady I work with owns his mother. She had a litter of four. He was the last to be adopted."

"I'm going to miss him," Dean lamented.

"Well, why don't you call me? You're welcome to come over and see him. The least I can do is have you visit him."

"By the way, how did you lose him?"

"I had an old, worn leash. We were walking in the woods behind the park. He just sort of broke away. I looked down and he was gone. Called and called his name, but no dog came. Unfortunately puppies don't leave footprints in the woods."

Katie stopped and each of them just looked at the other.

Dean spoke next. "Say, would you like to go out for a cup of coffee?"

Katie smiled from ear to ear. "Sure."

"Uh, we better not leave Sonny—I mean Sheriff—here. He howls and barks when left alone."

"That's okay, we can get coffee and drink in my car."

They went out to the car and to a drive-in nearby. Dean asked Katie what she'd like and returned, but Katie insisted he take a few dollars. "Please, after what you've done for me."

He returned and they began talking.

Dean started the conversation. "So, what kind of work do you do?"

"I'm a nurse. At the county hospital. Two years now."

"Oh, great. Do you live in town?"

"Right across from the hospital. There are a couple of apartment houses. A lot of hospital employees live there. You know, when working for a hospital you need to live nearby. You can get a call almost any time to come in."

"Yeah, I know that. But you need to have a social life."

"I do, but it's mostly with folks from the hospital."

"Have you got a boyfriend?"

"No. I did, but we broke up. Before my job at the hospital." She paused. "Unless you count Sheriff."

They both laughed. Dean halted for a few seconds, and looked out the window. He wanted to ask Katie for a date. He was always shy around girls. But it was now or never.

"Say, maybe we could go out for dinner one night. And a movie. If you care to go out with me, that is."

There was a sparkle and a flash in her eyes, as if she waited for him to ask.

She spoke softly. "Sure, that's wonderful. Two years at the hospital, I get most weekends off. How about this Saturday?"

Dean was overjoyed. He hadn't been on a date in years. "Any place in particular you'd like to go to?"

"I'll let you decide. You seem like you have good taste. You took good care of my dog. And your sign in the coffee shop caught my eye."

"Okay, I'll think of a good, cozy place we can go to."

Katie drove Dean home. When she got to the front of his home, she smiled warmly.

"Thanks again. You did a blessed thing for me."

"Oh, my pleasure. Besides, I love animals."

He kissed Katie on the cheek and petted Sheriff a few times. In his heart, he felt alone, in just a few days, he had grown very attached to the puppy. But in just a short time, he felt genuinely attached to Katie as well.

"Be sure to call me."

"I will," Dean promised. He stepped out from the car. And she drove away.

-6-

Dean faced a few more lonely, unemployed days. However, this week he had something to look forward to.

On Friday evening, the moment came that he waited eagerly for. He telephoned Katie.

"Hi, it's Dean."

"Oh, how wonderful to hear from you."

"How have you been? How's work at the hospital?"

"Oh, okay I guess. I mean, I like my work. But it's not my life."

"How's Sheriff?"

"He's doing fine. He's back home, in the bed I bought for him."

"Does he howl when left alone?"

"No. I suppose he did it at your house because he wasn't familiar with it."

"I forgot to give you the dog food I had for him. How about we go out tomorrow night and I can bring it over?"

Oh, that's great. I'm sure Sheriff would love to see you."

"What's a good time to come over?"

"Seven o'clock is okay." Wait a minute. You don't have a car. I'll pick you up."

"Are you sure you don't mind?"

"Do I mind? After how you helped me get my dog back to me, picking you up is no problem at all."

"Gee, thanks."

"So, I'll be over at seven."

Dean felt overjoyed once more. He was impatiently waiting for Saturday evening.

Saturday morning he got his hair cut and took some of his dress clothes, the few he had, and removed them from the closet. Like a teenager going to a prom, he compared pants and shirts, different combinations, maybe a tie. He was so excited.

At just about 6:30 PM Katie called to advise that she was leaving her home. Dean made one last comb of his hair and took every little piece of lint off his pants.

Katie arrived at just about seven o'clock. Dean gave her a great big smile and hello, and welcomed her in. "You sure are prompt."

"When you work in a hospital, you learn to be on time. Anyway, I'm off the job. I don't really want to talk about my work."

Dean nodded. He seemed to agree.

"Oh, how's my little buddy? Does he miss me?"

"I think so. He probably didn't know you by name. I asked him a few times. He kind of looked at me the way dogs do. But he wagged his tail, so that's likely a yes."

"Does he howl and bark when left alone?"

"No"

"A couple of my neighbors griped about it. You know, the ones who sit home all day watching who goes in and out. The busybodies who could tell you which day of the week Mrs. Pastorakis goes to the hairdresser or who got vertical blinds. They know how long I'm out of work better than I do."

"There are nosy neighbors everywhere. I have them, too. Only with me, I live right across from where I work. They know what time I start and finish."

Dean felt it was better to change the subject. "By the way, you look pretty good tonight."

"Thanks. So anyway, where would you like to go tonight?"

Katie pretended to ponder, but she knew all along where to go. Although she hadn't asked Dean much about his work, she had an idea he didn't have a steady job. He had done her a great service, getting her pup back to her. She knew that she owed him more than a ride home.

"How about Ciro's?"

It's a restaurant in the downtown area. Ironically, just a block away from where he had painted the week before.

"I've seen Ciro's. Never been there. I passed it last week."

They got in the car and were on their way. The downtown area was surprisingly crowded, but they had no difficulty getting a table.

Katie asked Dean about his work. He explained that he had been unemployed since losing his job at the video store. He told her about Cliff, his sister, niece and nephews. He had survived on odd jobs, and the little his mother had left him. He mentioned the paint job the week before.

Kate asked, "Is that where Dr. Wainer is moving?"

To his surprise, she knew the doctor. He was affiliated with the hospital she worked at. "He's been looking for a new place for many years. That's what he told me. The downtown area was once pretty depressed. He said it's had a revival and he's moving not just for more office space but business had picked up."

"Picked up? The video store went out of business."

But he knew what she meant. There has been a resurgence. Yet it came with a negative side. The restaurants, new hotel and fruit stores had invigorated the town. But many hired illegal aliens, and it cost some residents their jobs. Dean was one of them.

Katie agreed. Many were getting services at the hospital, and not paying for them.

Dean was curious how Katie knew what she did about town.

"I detect a slight accent in your speech. Never seen you in town until you came to get Sheriff. Is this your hometown? Did you go to school here?"

She went on to explain. "I'm originally from the Boston area. Then my family moved to Rhode Island I was eleven at the time. I studied nursing in Rhode Island.

Came to the Hudson Valley two years ago after seeing the job offer in a nursing newsletter. I was interning outside of Providence."

"Do you have family in Massachusetts or Rhode Island?"

Katie evaded the question. "I studied in Rhode Island. I didn't want to go back to Boston. The job here offered me more opportunities."

Dean looked at her quizzically, but could see she didn't want to elaborate. He liked her, and the relationship was getting off to a good start. Better to leave it as it was.

Dean spoke of his life in town, how many of his friends moved away, his parent's death. And his fond memories of playing in the park where Sheriff entered his life.

They finished dinner and walked around town. Holding hands, they passed the office where Dean had painted earlier in the week, and he also noticed a number of new cafes, a book store, florist. The downtown area had indeed rejuvenated. Dean had not been here much in the last year or so, but he was able to identify locations where there had once been an old factory, or a social club, a law office. Katie found it of interest. She knew little of town, despite a two year residency.

You know more about town than my coworkers," she boasted.

They walked back to the car.

"I'll bet you'd really like to see Sheriff again."

Dean was happy to hear that.

"Come on over. I'll make you coffee. Don't worry. I'll take you home."

Katie took him and Dean explained how many times he had passed the area in his youth. He pointed to where there had once been a record store, a gymnasium and bowling alley. She was impressed that where she lived had once been the location of a bowling alley, hardware store and parking lot.

They went to Katie's apartment, on the second floor of a three story unit. She opened the door, turned on the light, and the familiar charge of a puppy came running, jumping and leaping at Dean's leg. He picked the dog up and got a cascade of kisses.

Katie made coffee and gave Sheriff a couple of biscuits that Dean had left over. He spent about an hour and Katie drove him home. As she dropped him off, he asked about the possibility of another date.

"I think you know that I'd like to see you again. Besides, my dog wouldn't think too kindly to not seeing you any more."

"So I can call you again?"

"Definitely. I won't be off again until next weekend. But you can drop by one night next week."

They kissed and embraced. Dean felt like life was worthwhile again, a sensation he had not experienced in so, so long. As he entered the lobby, there was Krady emptying his garbage. Just a few days before, Dean would likely have waited until his cranky neighbor went back into his cage. But tonight, he held his head high and whistled, completely ignoring Krady.

On Tuesday night, Dean telephoned Katie. She explained when she'd finish her tour. He didn't want to take advantage. He took the bus into town and they met at the cafe where she saw his sign about the lost puppy.

They were at her apartment where he got to see Sheriff again. Sheriff sat on his lap as they watched television. Katie spoke to Dean about whether or not he had found full time or steady work.

"No," he said sadly. "There isn't much in town. I could probably get something in a fast food place or making donuts. But that's not what I want to do. I need something more professional. Something with potential for advancement. I can't flip burgers. I need something steady. My unemployment will expire soon."

He gave his thoughts, but didn't want to go on about it. He was enjoying the evening with Katie, until she broached a subject which obviously made him feel bad. The conversation switched to other topics. Then they made a date for Friday.

On Friday night Katie picked up Dean after her work. No work the next day, so she had time to talk at length with him.

"There's a medical clinic that needs a video technician. It's like a library for videotapes played at health fairs, seminars, schools, senior citizen's centers. You said you worked in a video store. I took the liberty of giving your name as being interested and qualified. Here's the number. You can call Monday."

Dean came close to tears, then hugged and held Katie tightly. In seconds, a few tears did come. Looking into her face, she cried also.

It had been so long since Dean felt any kind of emotion, warmth or gratitude. But he was experiencing love, and hope, feelings that had been absent for what seemed like ages.

It was nearly midnight when Katie drove him home. Being familiar with the medical videos, she offered to call him the next day to help him prepare for the interview.

"I'd value and appreciate your help. And I need a job, too."

The next afternoon Katie called and told him what the job would entail. She explained that his resume' need not be lengthy, just show experience with videos.

Early on Monday, Dean called and was asked if he could come in the same day for an interview. He promptly said yes.

The bus stop he got off at left him nearly half a mile from the clinic. But he used the walking time to review his job experience and any questions Katie told him to expect.

The clinic wasn't anything like he expected. The office he went into had no nurses, doctors or patients. No smell of a doctor's office, no one in white uniforms. He was in a medical records office.

The receptionist looked up as Dean gave his name and reason for being there. "Oh, yes, Miss Votello said you were proficient in video storage." Votello, he knew Katie's surname was something like that. He never knew exactly how to write or say it.

The wait for the interview took longer than he expected. Several times the receptionist explained that the supervisor who'd be conducting the interview was busy. He saw the secretary go into the office, and each time he was expecting her to say that it would be just a few more minutes. He looked at her and she looked his way cautiously, giving him the impression that the interviewer had asked about him. Was he getting impatient, was he neat and well dressed, did he look like a man who could do the job? Maybe there was another candidate in ahead of him, someone who really struck the boss as qualified, experienced and intelligent. Maybe the interviewer was evaluating him from behind a peephole. All kinds of thoughts went through Dean's mind. He was getting impatient, but tried his best not to show it. That was all he had to do, and his chances of being hired would diminish. Not just that, but he'd let Katie down. She had gone out of her way to help him land the job. He couldn't mess it up now.

Finally, the door opened and a man who appeared to be just about Dean's age came out of the office. Speaking for just a moment with the receptionist, he approached Dean in a friendly but official way.

"Good morning, I'm Mr. Cole, video library supervisor. Come into the office, please."

A few seconds of absolute silence. Then Cole spoke. "Your name, sir?"

"Dean Hollins" A bit of hesitation. "I've got a resume', sir."

Mr. Cole extended his hand and Dean presented the resume'. Cole perused it for a few minutes.

"Are you familiar with video libraries?'

"Yes, I am."

"Caring for videos, making copies, storing them?"

"Yes, I indicated such on the resume', as you may have read."

Cole pressed his lips, put his glasses on again, reread the resume', then looked at the candidate. "You seem to have experience. Come with me, I'll show you our library and conference rooms."

Dean followed Mr. Cole down what seemed like a hall a mile long. Cole opened a door marked video library, and ushered Dean in.

He was livid if not dumbfounded. Never in his life had he seen so many tapes. The video store had nothing like this.

"This is our library. These tapes are used by our medical staff. We also have tapes from medical associations, doctors, seminars. Some are educational tapes. We have students come in to view them. Some students come here on class trips, also senior citizen's groups. And therapy groups like stop smoking, losing weight, good nutrition. We make copies and send tapes to colleges, medical schools, boards of health, and so on. The librarian is responsible for sending out and keeping records of where they go and when they are due back. As you can see, we have hundreds of books as well."

Dean frankly admitted he saw a large number of tapes and asked how many in the library.

"There are upwards of 11,000. The county medical association took the initiative of having a large number of tapes to make this a first class hospital. It brings in business, we have conferences here and it gives us a good name. As you can imagine, there's a lot of responsibility in maintaining these tapes and books. The librarian's attention to tape requests reflects on the hospital's reputation."

Cole encouraged Dean to look at the tapes and books. "At times, you'll be asked to give an introduction or a presentation, so your speaking skills are important as well."

Dean stood tall and replied, "Oh, certainly. I can do that very well."

"Yes, I was told you can. We've got DVDs as well. They must be cared for, arranged and cared for like the tapes and books."

Mr. Cole then took Dean further down the hall and showed him the conference rooms and video equipment where tapes and DVDs could be copied or packaged for shipment. "Let's return to my office."

Dean sat again, trying to determine if he had made a good impression. It was hard to tell. Mr. Cole gave no indication of how he felt or rated Dean. If anything, Dean was more uncertain now than he had been when he first walked in.

"You come with a good recommendation. You appear bright and responsible. There are a few other points you must understand. This is mostly a nine to five job, but there are days you'll have to stay later. We have some evening seminars. Does that pose a conflict?"

Dean assured he could work an occasional evening.

Cole gave his first real sign of approval. "Very well. You've got thirty days probation, but you seem intelligent and you're hired. When can you start?"

Dean offered to begin working at any time. Mr. Cole asked him to be ready to start the following Monday. Salary and benefits were discussed.

Mr. Cole congratulated him with a firm handshake as Dean gave the brightest smile he had shone in so long.

Later that evening, he called Katie with the good news. She screamed a yell of victory, as Dean thanked her for the kind words she had put in.

"Well, I guess this means a celebration. You and I. And Sheriff."

That Saturday night Katie picked Dean up and they went to dinner, followed by dancing and a night parked on a lane overlooking the Hudson. Afterwards, they returned to Katie's apartment where they spent their first night together.

The job was not a very lucrative one, but he was earning a salary and he felt like there was value to his life. He saw Katie often at the clinic, and every weekend.

Seven months passed as Dean did well on the job and Mr. Cole was extremely happy with his work. Dean was promoted to chief video librarian. He continued dating Katie, by now they were together several nights each week.

And each time Sheriff was there also. Sheriff just loved when Dean came around, he thought of both as his parents. Many times when Dean and Katie went out for a day, a walk in the park, or a ride to the campground, Sheriff went with them.

It was nearly eight months, and Dean felt more than just looking forward to seeing Katie. He was lonely and lost on the nights she worked late or when they were not together.

One day Mr. Cole asked Dean to stay late for a medical conference. It was on short notice, an evening when Dean had planned to visit Katie. Dean hesitated saying no to Mr. Cole. Cole had been good to him and often let him leave early or allow him to go to the hospital to have lunch with Katie. So he agreed to stay for the conference.

Katie understood, despite the fact that she had worked the weekend to cover nurses that were unable to report to work, and stayed late the following two days. Both had been looking forward to a quiet evening together. But Katie wasn't one to let disappointment stand in her way. If they couldn't spend the night together at her place, she'd go to his job. And just as the conference was about to begin, in walked Katie. She wasn't an invited guest, but Mr. Cole allowed her to stay in the audience. And her presence made working late all the more worthwhile.

In his heart he felt what had escaped him for years and years. He loved Katie, but also sensed a need for her, a desire to be with her. Whether it was a movie, or dinner, to shop, or a walk through the neighborhood with Sheriff on a leash, the hours he spent with her were unlike any others. He didn't just love her, he needed her. No one else made him feel so wanted or needed.

Dean's sister Cheryl noticed the difference as well. There was a smile in his voice, optimism in his reports.

Cheryl asked if he felt he had met the right girl. She reminded him that their parents had warned them not to rush into any major decisions. But she also told him that he had spent much of his time alone. His life had been unstable, he was lonely and had little ambition until he had met Katie. Did he feel the time for marriage had come, and more vital, was Katie the right girl for him?

Only he could make the decision. It was time for him to confront it. The next time he'd see Katie would be Saturday. He wanted a special evening. But as Dean saw it, this would not be one where he'd wine and dine her expensively, or wear his finest clothes. No distractions, no illusions. In all this time he had come to know Katie well. When something of importance needed to be discussed, he could relate to her best on an honest and open level. No drapes to hide the stage.

He got to Katie's apartment at 3 PM, and while she was still working, he bought a bouquet of flowers. That was as far as the extravagance would go for the occasion.

If he was going to ask her to marry him, he wanted her to answer without anything that made it like a ruse to tempt her.

It was just after 5:30 PM when Katie arrived home. The calendar said June, but the shades were closed and the lights were out. She walked in and as she saw the flowers, she gasped. Overjoyed, she came close to crying, when Dean came out of the kitchen, he saw her reaction, and could tell she was in the frame of mind he wanted. Flowers would get her attention more than an expensive dinner. She looked at him, and did so like she never did before.

Emerging from the semi-darkness, with almost a silhouette of light around him, he stood frozen for a moment. And she fixed her attention on him, as he did on her. She looked, and she was still, fixated on the man she met many months before when she went to obtain her lost dog. In the course of a few minutes, all they had shared since that first call she made to inquire about the puppy, replayed and replayed.

She put down her bag. He entered the room closer to her, where there was more light. Gradually they approached each other, held hands, as she lay her head on his shoulder.

In that position they remained for what seemed like a quarter of an hour. They then moved to the couch, they sat, held hands, and gazed at each other. And during all this time not a word was spoken. Not one sound. Sheriff would otherwise have done what he always did, jump on her and kiss her as dogs are prone to do. But he, too, in perhaps a way only a dog could understand, kept his distance. He was just a dog, but he had the canine intuition which told him to stay away, just for a little while. This was his masters' time, and he stayed in the bedroom, wagging his tail, waiting for the right moment to run out.

Dean had rehearsed his words and anticipated her possible responses, but at this point he realized all his fears and uncertainties had been for naught. The moment had come.

Katie held his hand and cried as she stroked her hair, whispered and smiled broadly. Dean did not have to give any explanations, or ask any questions. He looked, cried and whispered along with her. "Yes, I'll marry you," she spoke as he never asked her the way he planned it. And at that very moment, Sheriff came running into the room, and jumped onto their laps.

In a few months they were Mr. and Mrs. and all made possible when a mischievous Labrador retriever broke away from his leash in the woods one year before.

CPSIA information can be obtained at www.ICGtesting.com
Printed in the USA
BVOW08s2322150715

408997BV00003B/29/P